Practical Hi[...] on playing th[...]

ALTO SAXOPHONE

by Eugene Rousseau
in collaboration with James D. Ployhar

Foreword

The *"Practical Hints"* series is a unique and highly informative set of books designed to answer the many important questions raised by the beginning musician as well as the more advanced student.

Each book has been prepared by a nationally known instrumental specialist and covers such vital topics as CARE AND MAINTENANCE, REEDS AND MOUTHPIECES, PLAYING POSITION, EMBOUCHURE, TUNING, TONGUING, TONE QUALITY and RANGE as well as the methodology of PRACTICE.

Every book contains a number of pictures along with practical playing exercises designed to rapidly improve basic musicianship.

The *"Practical Hints"* series may be used along with the FIRST DIVISION BAND COURSE, the CONTEMPORARY BAND COURSE or any other recognized band method. An appropriate book from this series should be in every young musicians' library as a companion book to the method.

The books in the *"Practical Hints"* series are for individual use only and may not be played together in a band class. Books are published separately for the following instruments:

Published for:

FLUTE
B♭ CLARINET
ALTO CLARINET
BASS CLARINET
OBOE
BASSOON
ALTO SAXOPHONE
TENOR SAXOPHONE
BARITONE SAXOPHONE
CORNET/TRUMPET
FRENCH HORN
TROMBONE
BARITONE (Euphonium)
TUBA (Bass)
PERCUSSION (Snare Drum, Bass Drum, Timpani, Cymbals)
MALLET PERCUSSION

EL 2706

About the Author

One of the great saxophonists of the world, Eugene Rousseau has had an extensive background in classical as well as jazz music. Since his highly successful solo debut in New York's Carnegie Hall he has had engagements throughout the world, including the countries of Canada, England, France, Germany, Holland, Austria, New Zealand, Australia, Africa, and Japan, in addition to covering all quarters of the United States. He possesses a wide knowledge in the area of woodwind instruments which he has used thoroughly during the course of his professional playing and teaching career. He earned the Ph.D. from the University of Iowa in 1962, and has been Professor of Music at Indiana University since 1964, having served as Chairperson of the Woodwind Department for six years at the latter institution.

Rousseau has recorded numerous solo works for saxophone, including an album of concertos on the Deutsche Grammophon label. Among his publications are a two-volume *Method for Saxophone* (Kjos), and a work on the above-normal range of the saxophone, *Saxophone High Tones* (Etoile), as well as numerous solos and arrangements. Over the past decade Eugene Rousseau has devoted a large share of his creative ability to the artistic and acoustical development of saxophones and saxophone mouthpieces. As Chief Consultant to the Yamaha Corporation for saxophone research and development, he has made 18 trips to Japan during the past ten years.

From 1978 until 1980 he served as the elected President of the North American Saxophone Alliance.

Contents

Unit I. Care and Cleaning

Study carefully the parts of the saxophone shown in photo No. 1. Each part has an important job to do in making your saxophone play its best. But, for all these parts to work their best for you, you must take a few minutes each day to give your instrument the kind of care it needs. Remember, the finest professional saxophonists do not play an instrument that is not in good working order. You might also keep in mind the old saying, "An ounce of prevention is worth a pound of cure." Take your saxophone to a reliable repair shop for a check-up each six months. Between check-up times you should follow the helpful suggestions given below.

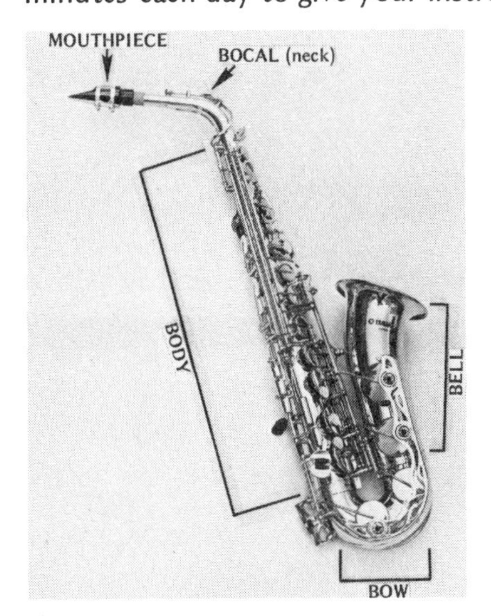

Photo No. 1.

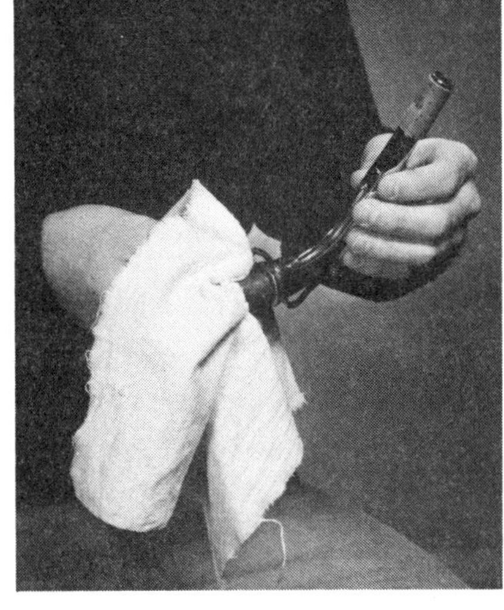

Photo No. 2.

A soft, clean cloth should be used to wipe your saxophone after each use. This is the best way to care for the finish. Polishing cloths that have strong chemicals in them are not recommended for lacquered finishes. Be careful in wiping your saxophone so that neither the cloth nor your fingers get caught on the sharp springs. A separate, clean cloth should be used to absorb the excess moisture from inside the bocal and also from inside the top of the body. Photo Nos. 2 and 3.

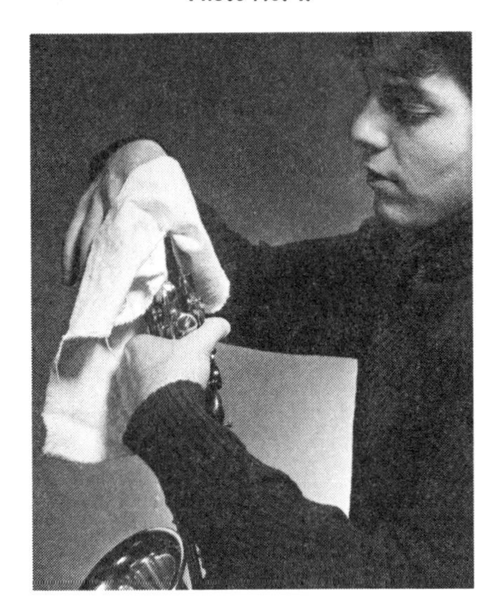

Photo No. 3.

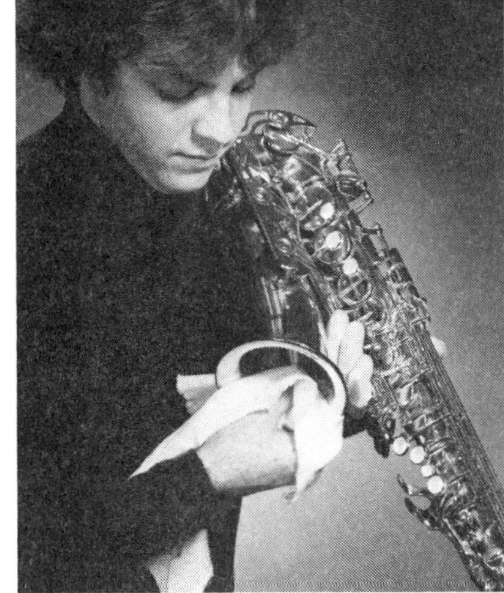

Photo No. 4.

When you have finished playing, remove the bocal and wipe it out. Tip your saxophone upside down so that any excess moisture may run out. Then, carefully wipe the bell with a soft cloth so that the water drops will not stain the finish. Photo No. 4.

A very, very small amount of key oil should be used on the moving parts of your saxophone every 30 or 60 days. You and your teacher might like to mark these important dates on the calendar. Use *very little* oil. If too much oil is used it will eventually get on the pads of your saxophone, causing them to stick and to attract dirt. Excess oil can also get on your fingers, making playing your instrument uncomfortable. Photo No. 5.

Photo No. 5.

Photo No. 6.

Some professionals use swabs for absorbing the moisture from their saxophones after playing. This is not absolutely necessary. If you do use a swab, however, be certain that it is one that does not give off lint that could clog the tone-holes, or stick to the pads. If a pad becomes sticky it may be blotted several times with a clean cloth to remove the sticky substance. Photo No. 6.

Unit II. The Reed and Mouthpiece

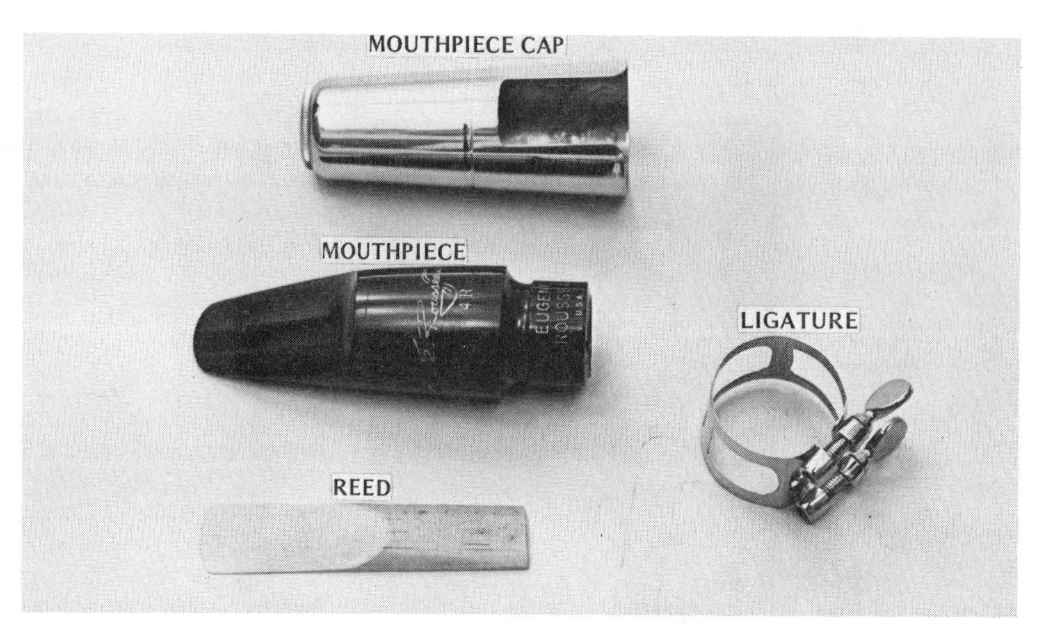

Photo No. 7.

Several methods may be used to give your reed and mouthpiece proper care, but here are the most important points to follow: (1) Take the reed off the mouthpiece after each time you have played. Wipe it carefully with your thumb and index finger. If possible, hold the reed under running water for a few seconds, then wipe it. Photo No. 8.

(2) Pull a small cloth through your mouthpiece. An old cotton handkerchief is ideal for this purpose. This will keep your mouthpiece in the best condition for getting the best tone and response. A mouthpiece that is not cleaned regularly will become clogged with dirt. A mouthpiece in this condition is much more difficult to play. Besides, who wants to play on a dirty mouthpiece? Photo No. 9.

(3) After cleaning your mouthpiece and reed you may put the reed back on the mouthpiece, but do not tighten the screws of the ligature. Then, put the mouthpiece cap on. Or, you may put the reed back in a cardboard holder. Some performers keep their reeds in special metal holders when they are not playing. This is not necessary, but you may decide upon such a holder after talking it over with your teacher. The most important things to remember are to be careful with your reed and mouthpiece, and to keep them clean.

It is best to use reeds of a medium strength, approximately No. 2½. Always have at lease two reeds ready to play. Do not use the same reed day after day. Alternate your reeds so that they will last longer. It is easy to keep track of your reeds by marking them with a pencil.

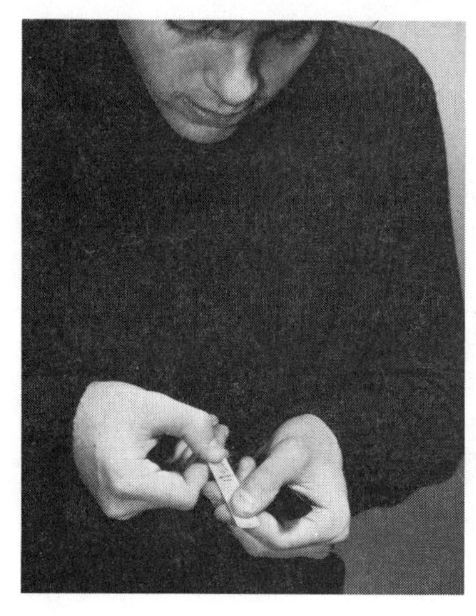

Photo No. 8.

Photo No. 9.

Photo No. 10.

Mouthpieces are available in many shapes and in several kinds of materials. In order to achieve the highest level of success in your playing you should use a *medium facing* mouthpiece made of hard rubber. *Facing* is a term used to describe the curve of the mouthpiece. This curve is most important because it determines how your reed will vibrate. Photo No. 11.

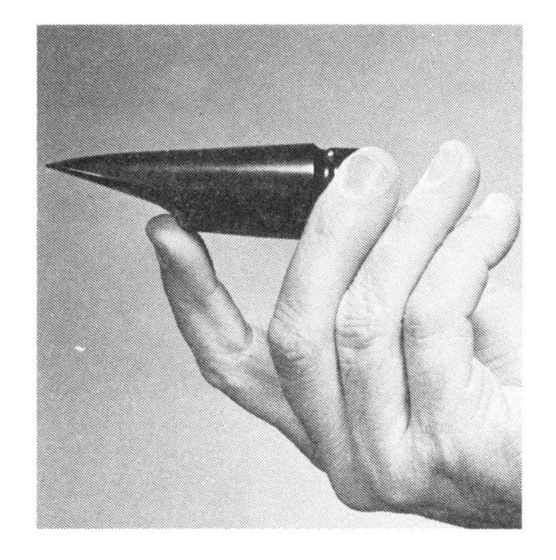

Photo No. 11.

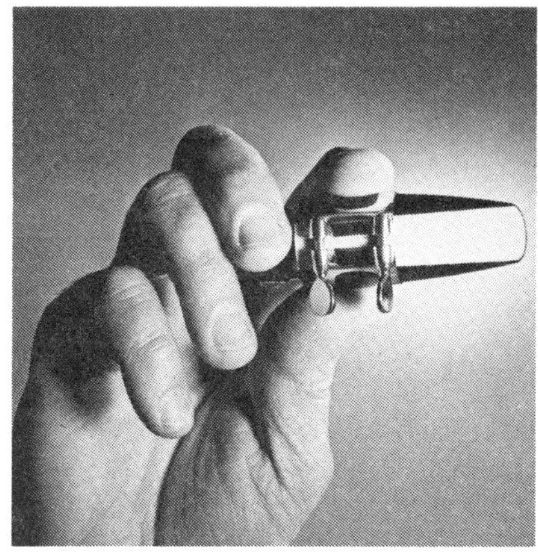

Photo No. 12.

Always begin playing by having your reed even with the tip of the mouthpiece, or just slightly below the tip. At most there should be just a line of black showing as you hold the reed and mouthpiece at eye level. Photo No. 12.

Tighten the ligature until it is firm, but do not make it extremely tight.

Unit III. Playing Position

Study the pictures so that you will know the correct and incorrect ways to hold the alto saxophone. Notice that in the sitting position there are two ways to hold your instrument. You should use the way that is most comfortable for you. Study the curved position of each hand. The cushions of the finger tips are used to close the keys. Do not let your fingers overlap the keys. Photo Nos. 13, 14 and 15.

Photo No. 13 – Correct.

Photo No. 14 – Correct.

Photo No. 15 – Incorrect.

You should sit forward in your chair. Do not rest against the back of your chair while playing. Sit up straight. When you have several measures rest you may relax and rest your back against the back of the chair. Keep the saxophone forward if you hold it on the right side. It should rest against the side of your leg, not against the chair. In this way you will be able to see your band director, and you will also be able to take a good breath.

If you hold your alto saxophone directly in front of you, between your legs, do not rest it on the chair. Sit forward, let the instrument come to you. Remember to let the weight of the saxophone rest on the neck strap. Do *not* support the weight of the saxophone with your right thumb. If you do, your hands will become tired and tense, and you will not develop as a good player. Photo Nos. 16, 17 and 18.

Photo No. 16 – Correct – The saxophone is coming to the player.

Photo No. 17 -Incorrect – The saxophone is too low.

Photo No. 18 – Incorrect – The saxophone is too low. The player is going to the saxophone.

Photo No. 19.

Photo No. 20.

In the standing position you must also let the saxophone come to you. Notice that the instrument rests against the right front part of the player's body. This gives another point for balancing the saxophone so that it will be stable while you are standing and playing. Photo No. 19.

You may turn the mouthpiece and move the bocal so that the saxophone will come to you more easily. You should sit or stand in a comfortable position, then adjust the neck strap, mouthpiece, and bocal so the saxophone will come to you. Photo No. 20.

Unit IV. The Alto Saxophone Embouchure

Look very carefully at the photos below. You will see the correct and an incorrect embouchure. The correct embouchure for the alto saxophone will feel *round,* and will support the reed and mouthpiece with a circular feeling. Photo Nos. 21, 22, 23 and 24.

Photo No. 21 – Correct.

Photo No. 22 – Correct.

Photo No. 23 – Incorrect.

Photo No. 24 – Incorrect.

After you have carefully placed the reed on the mouthpiece, play the following exercise using the alto saxophone MOUTHPIECE ONLY.

NOTE: This exercise is given in *concert pitch* (your teacher will explain).

CONCERT PITCH – Count slowly.

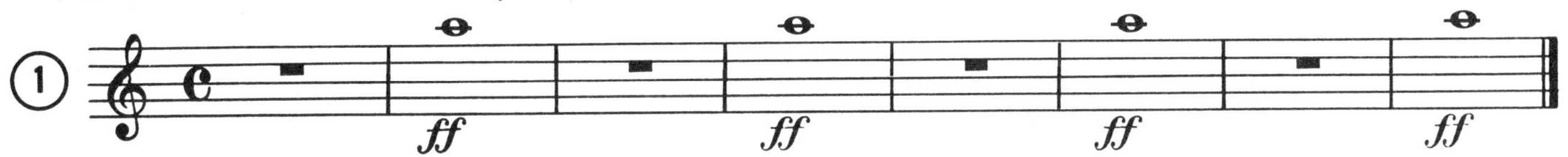

Put the mouthpiece on your saxophone; play the following exercise with the same embouchure and same feeling used in ①.

Count slowly.

NOTE: Only exercise ① is given in concert pitch.

Play the exercises below using the same embouchure and same feeling as used in ①. Be sure that your mouthpiece is at the proper position on the bocal of your saxophone (see Unit V).

Count slowly. Keep your embouchure firm.

Count slowly. Do not move your jaw.

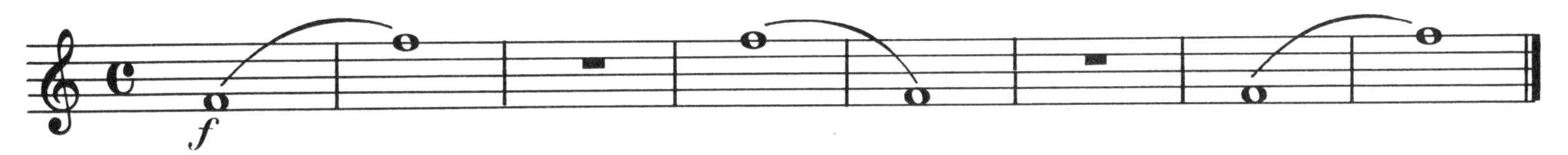

Count slowly.

Do not move your jaw.

Keep your embouchure firm.

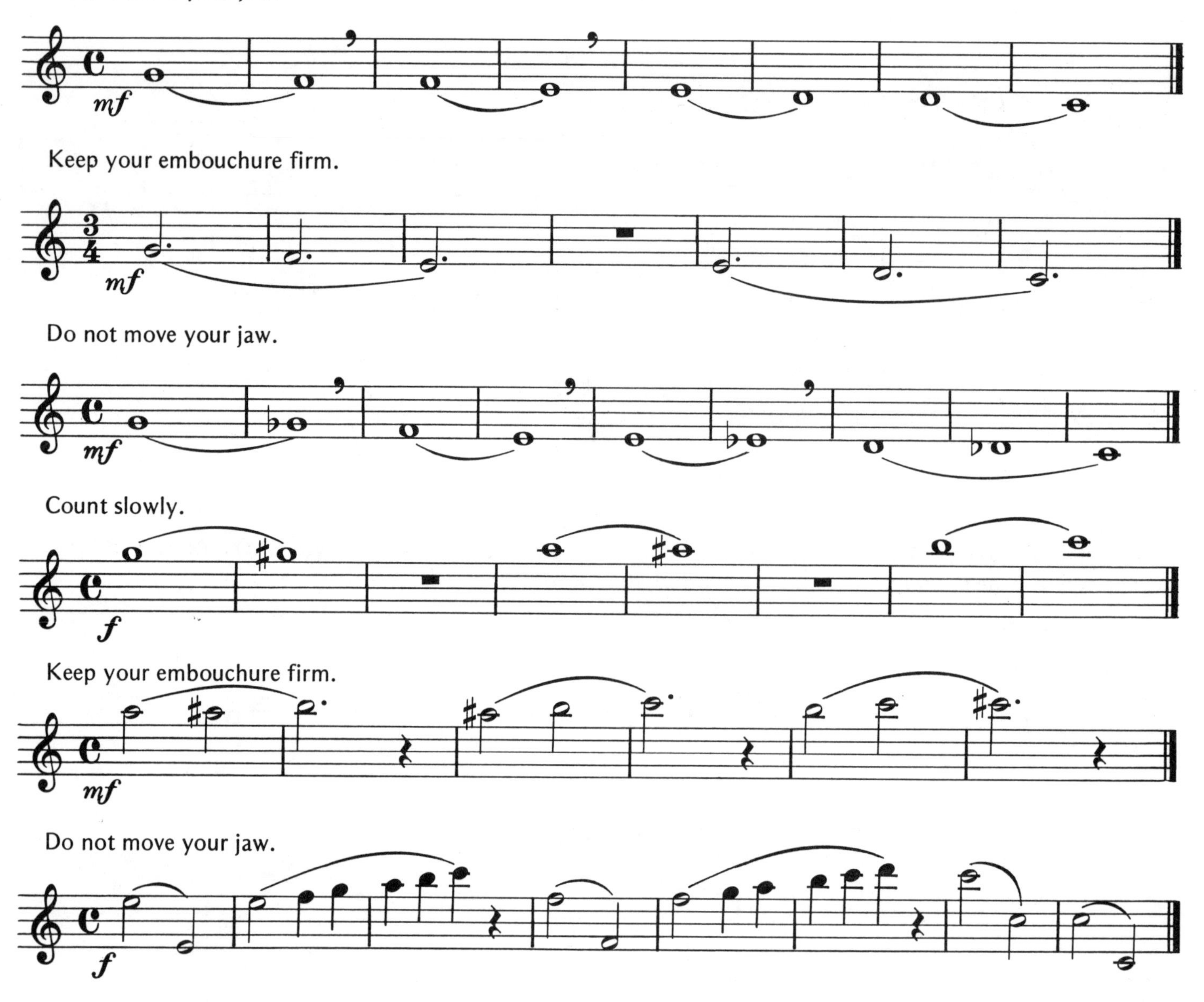

Unit V. Pitch, Tuning and Intonation

Pitch refers to how high or how low you play.

Tuning refers to adjusting your saxophone to play higher or lower.

Intonation (playing in tune) refers to the pitch of your saxophone after you have tuned. The information and exercises below will help you to understand the *pitch, tuning,* and *intonation* of your alto saxophone. *Tuning* your instrument to the proper *pitch* is important because it helps you (1) to play better in tune with other instruments, (2) to play better in tune with your own instrument, and (3) to get a better tone quality.

The tuning of your alto saxophone is done by adjusting the position of the mouthpiece on the bocal (neck). If you make the saxophone longer, by pulling the mouthpiece out, you will make the pitch lower. If you make the saxophone shorter, by pushing the mouthpiece on, you will make the pitch higher. on the alto saxophone is concert A . This is a good note for tuning your saxophone because it is quite stable.

After tuning, make a mark on the cork to show the position of the mouthpiece on the bocal. Put your mouthpiece at this mark each time you assemble your saxophone. Photo Nos. 25 and 26.

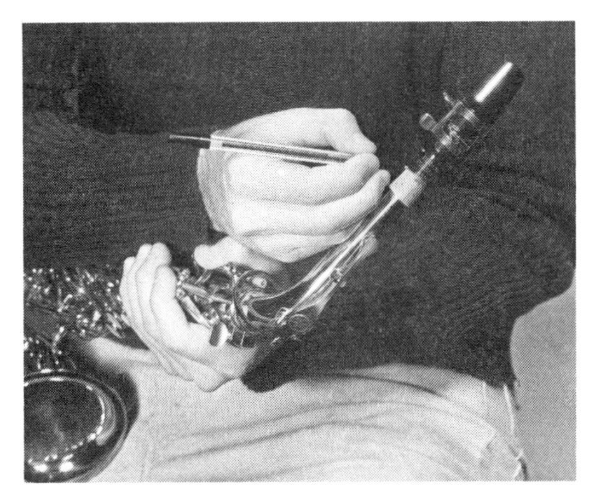

Photo No. 25.

Photo No. 26.

Remember to use the correct embouchure when tuning. Remember also that tuning does not guarantee good intonation; you must always listen carefully to your pitch. Some notes on the alto saxophone can be troublesome by being too high (sharp) or too low (flat). These notes are given below. They are troublesome for most alto saxophones, but not necessarily for all alto saxophones.

Play the following exercise with another alto saxophonist playing the second part. Or, the second part may be played on a well-tuned piano (small notes). Listen carefully. Use a good embouchure.

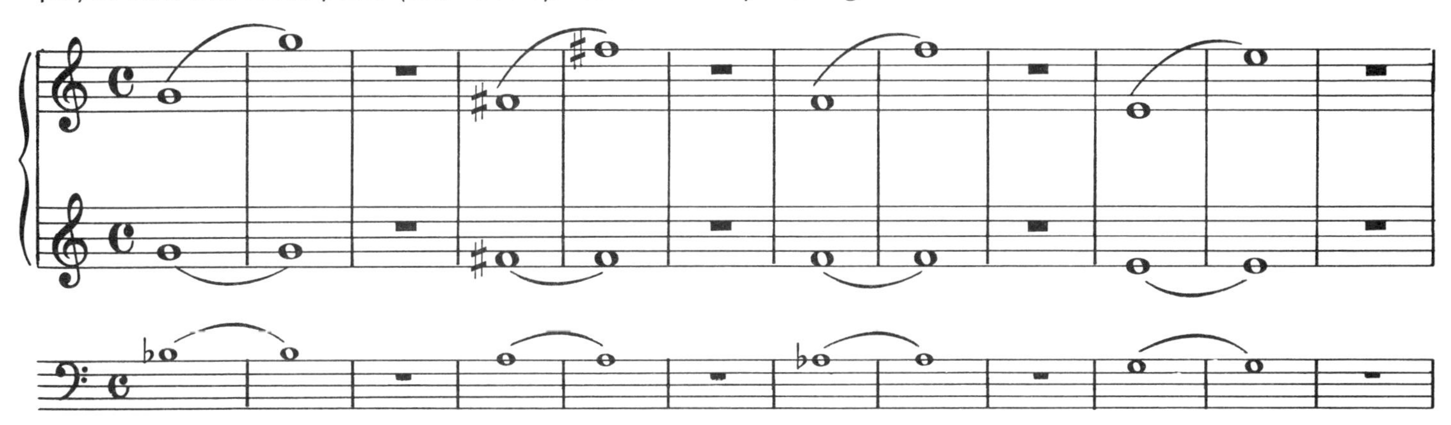

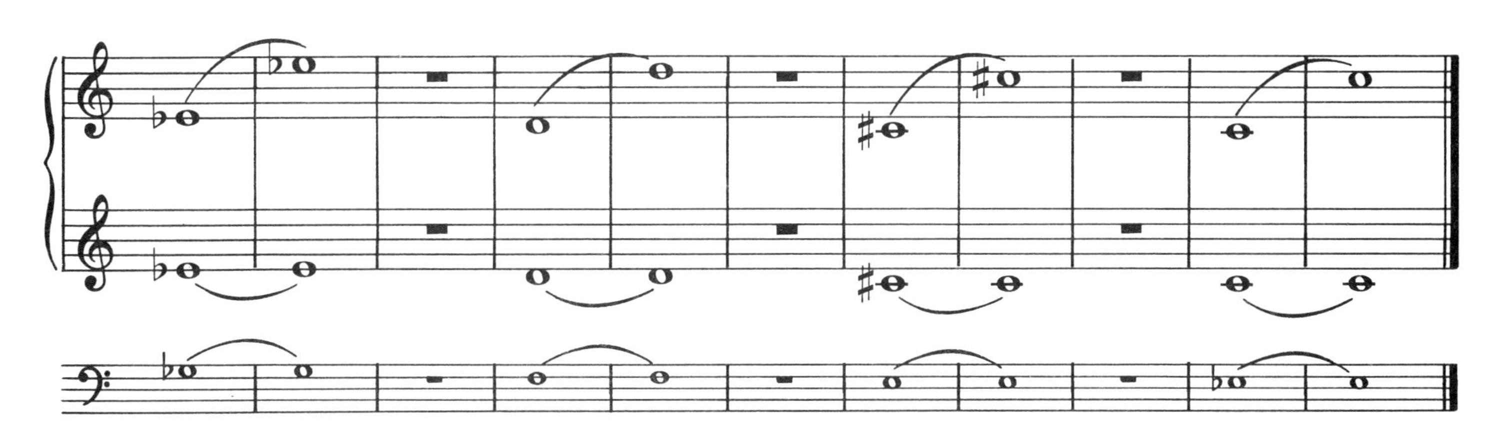

Play the following exercises with another alto saxophonist playing the second part. Or, the second part may be played on a well-tuned piano (small notes). Listen carefully. Use a good emouchure.

Unit VI. Breathing

Always breathe as deeply as possible and as quickly as possible through the corners of your mouth. Here are some helpful suggestions for developing good breathing: (Photo No. 27)

1. Keep your teeth on top of the mouthpiece.
2. Do not drop your jaw — keep your embouchure set.
3. Raise your upper lip just enough to breathe through the corners of your mouth.
4. Breathe quickly, and as deeply as possible.

Before playing each day, practice the following exercise:

5. Take a quick, deep breath — hold it for ten seconds.
6. Exhale.
7. Relax.

Photo No. 27.

After relaxing for a few seconds, do the following:

8. Take three quick breaths – one after the other. (Remember, breathe quickly and deeply) hold this breath for ten seconds.
9. Exhale.
10. Relax.

Repeat steps 5, 6, and 7 of the breathing exercise, but this time try to get the feeling of the amount of air taken in step 8. Practice steps 5 through 10 each day before playing. Then, do the following exercises before you begin to practice your assignments.

Count slowly. Keep the tone steady. Take a quick, deep breath.

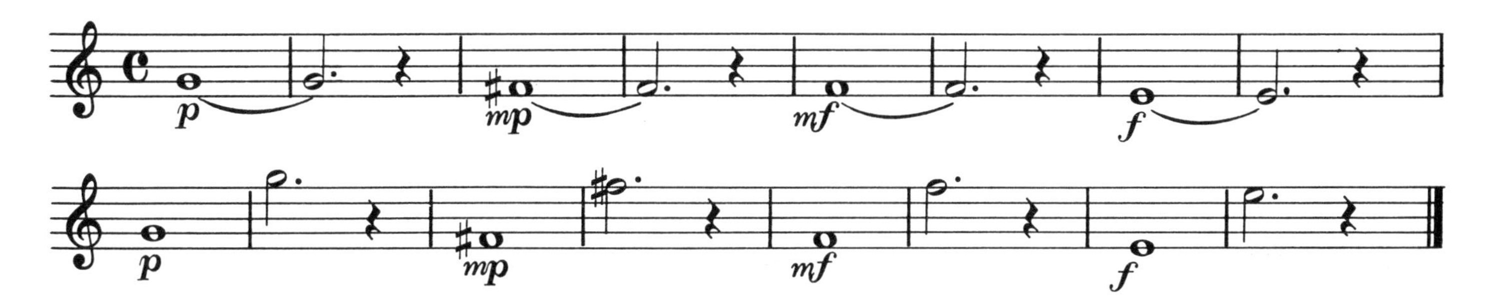

Slowly. Take a quick, deep breath. Keep your teeth on top of the mouthpiece. Make the *cresc.* gradually.

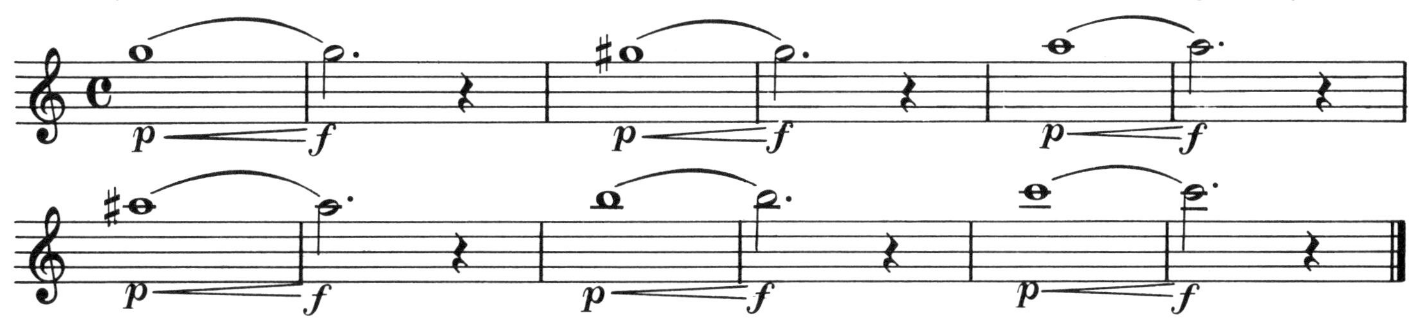

Slowly. Take a quick, deep breath. Keep your teeth on top of the mouthpiece. Make the *decesc.* gradually.

Slowly. Take a quick, deep breath. Keep your embouchure firm. Keep your teeth on top of the mouthpiece.

Keep your tone steady.

Take a quick, deep breath.

Keep your embouchure firm.

Move the fingers quickly, but do not rush the tempo.

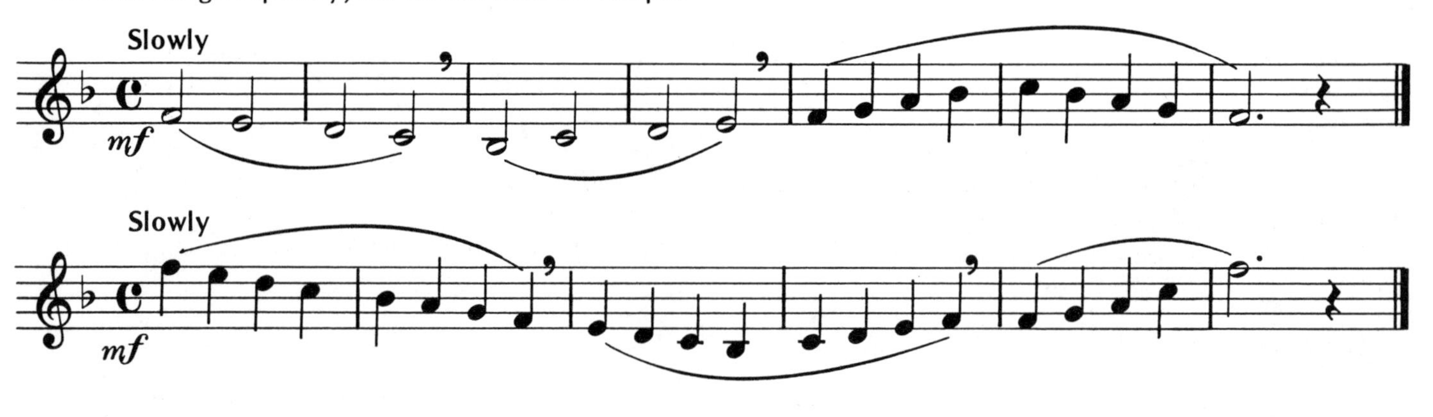

Keep your tone steady.

Slowly
Play as far as you can in one breath.
Breathe quickly and deeply.

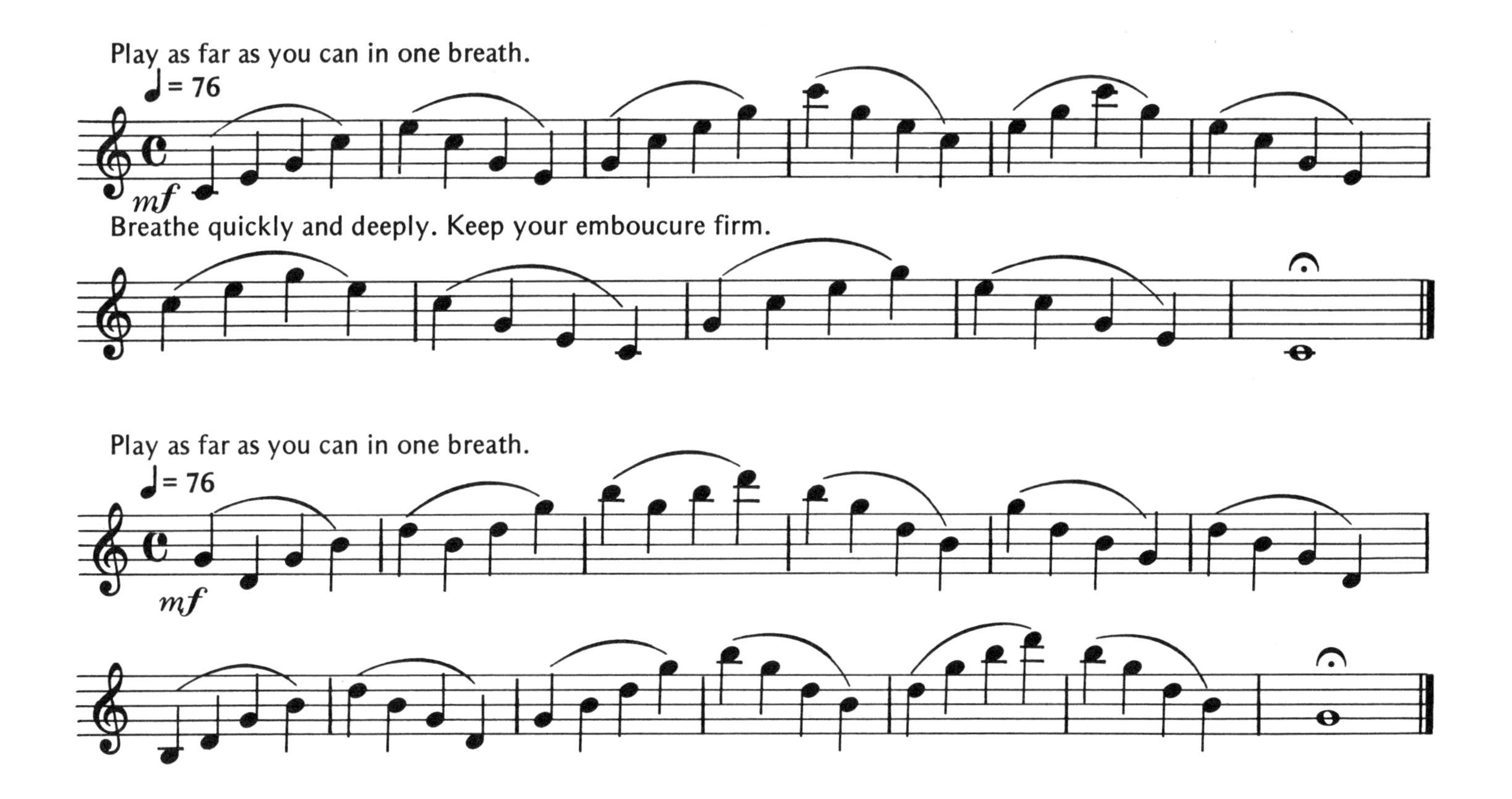

Play as far as you can in one breath.
♩= 76
mf
Breathe quickly and deeply. Keep your emboucure firm.
Play as far as you can in one breath.
♩= 76
mf

Unit VII. Tonguing

While playing the saxophone, if you touch the reed with your tongue you will stop the tone. When you take your tongue away from the reed while blowing, the tone will begin. This action of the tongue is called *tonguing* or *articulation.*

In order to begin a tone clearly, tonguing should be as natural as possible. Use the syllable DAH without having the mouthpiece in your mouth. Now put the mouthpiece in your mouth with the correct embouchure. Whisper DAH. The place where your tongue and reed make contact is the most natural for you. This is where you should tongue notes while playing the saxophone.

Play with AH only. Do not tongue.

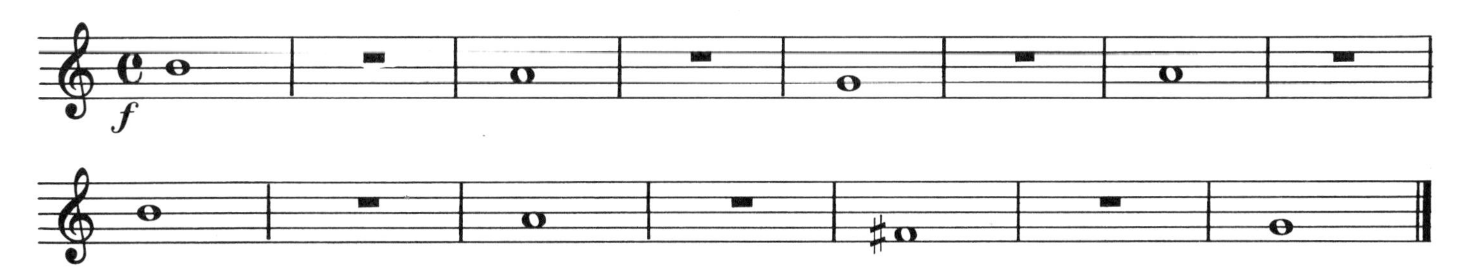

Play the following as marked. Tongue every other note.

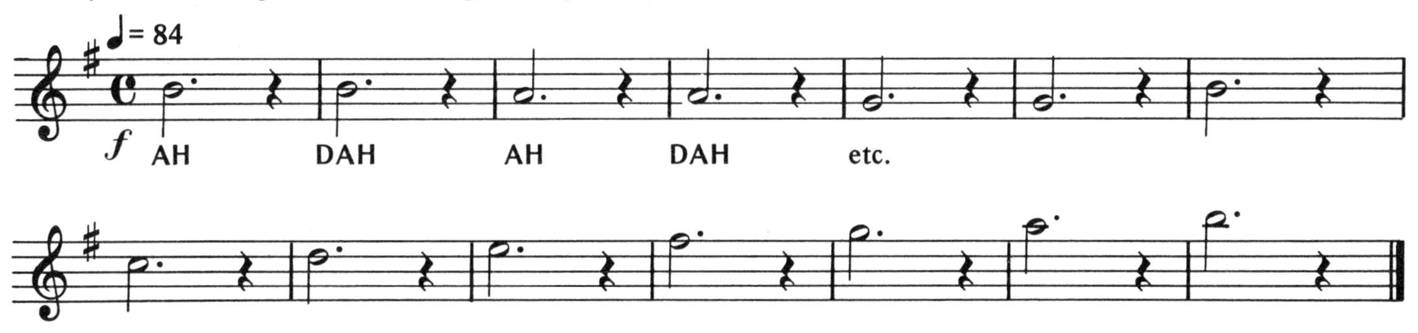

Remember that the AH is the tone, not the D.
♩= 120
f
DAH DAH DAH DAH DAH, etc.
Keep your embouchure firm for all the notes.
f
Use DAH.
♩= 92
f DAH DAH
♩= 104
mf
♩= 72
f
mf
f
mf

The above examples are called *legato tonguing*, which is usually used for pieces that do not move quickly. When notes must be tongued quickly, *staccato tonguing* is used. Often, the *staccato* is indicated by a dot above or below the notes. Notice that the syllable is now TAH.

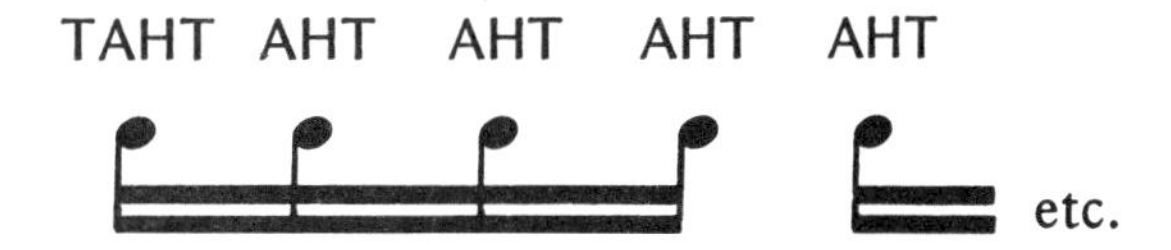

In staccato tonguing where notes are played quickly one after the other, the end of the first tone (T) becomes the beginning of the second tone.

Staccato notes are indicated by a dot above or below the note. Legato notes are indicated by a line above or below the note. Practice the following:

Do not add the T to the final note of a group. Use TAH, not TAHT, when playing the final note.

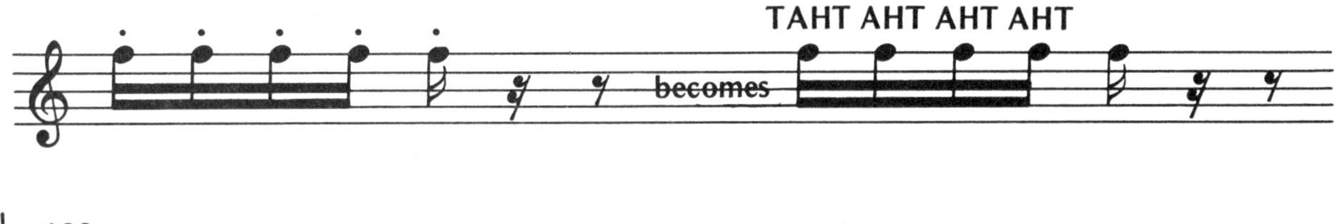

Keep your embouchure firm. Breathe quickly and deeply.

Unit VIII. Tone Quality and Range

A good tone quality is achieved by a combination of several important points. These are:

1. A good instrument in good condition (UNIT I).
2. A good embouchure (UNIT IV).
3. Proper breathing (UNIT VI).
4. Good practice habits (UNIT IX).
5. A good *concept* of tone.

Turn back and carefully re-read the sections on *Care and Maintenance* (UNIT I), *Embouchure* (UNIT IV), and *Breathing* (UNIT VI). Then study UNIT IX on *Practicing.* These Units cover four of the five points necessary for playing with a good tone quality. All five points are important. This Unit will discuss the *concept* of tone, and how you can make all five points work together to play with a good tone.

Concept of tone is a term used to describe an idea of a tone, or a picture of a tone that is in the mind of the player. This idea or picture can only be set in your mind by hearing a tone. That is why it is so important to listen to the best possible saxophone tones. There are many different good tones that you can hear by listening to good players. If you do not have the opportunity to hear a good player you can listen to one or more of the many fine recordings available today. Your teacher can help you to develop a good concept of tone.

As you develop a good concept of tone, you must know more about the quality of tone and range of your instrument. The alto saxophone range may be divided into four parts.

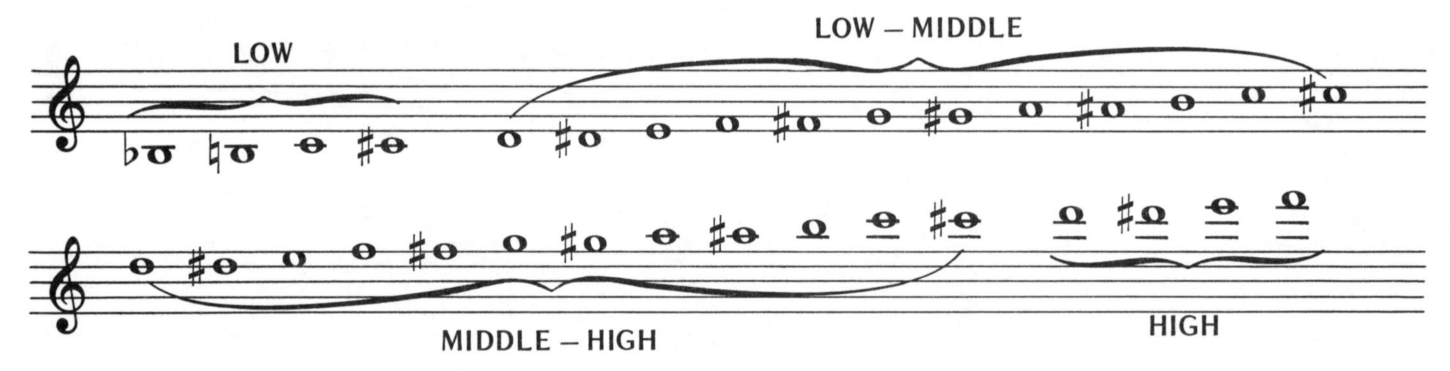

Each of these four parts has unique characteristics. In order to develop a good tone quality these parts must fit together smoothly. We must avoid sudden changes in tone quality as we play from one part of the range to another. The exercises below will help you to develop a smooth and even tone quality throughout the entire range of the alto saxophone.

2
3
4
5
6
7
Use the C-sharp fingering shown in no. 6.
8
9

10
11
12
13
14
g
15
16
Do not move your jaw. Keep your embouchure firm.
17
18

Unit IX. Practicing

No progress can be made without practicing. This comment is made often to young players, and by young players. Yet, too often, players do not know how to practice effectively. The steps given below will help you get the most out of every minute of your practicing. Read them carefully!

1. Daily practice
2. Goals in practicing
3. Practice plan
4. Practice time
5. Practice techniques

Daily practice: It is important to practice each day so that you can learn as quickly and as effectively as possible. Whenever there is a new idea to learn, *daily* practice is the best way to learn it. Daily practice cannot be made up. In other words, if you skip two or three days of practicing, you cannot make up the time by practicing three times as much during one day. Also, daily practice helps you to retain what you have already learned.

Goals in practicing: Both you and your teacher want to hear progress in your playing, of course! As you practice each day, try to improve at least one thing about your playing, no matter how small it may be. In other words, always have a goal in mind while you are practicing.

Practice plan: You must have a plan in order to achieve your goals. Many players call this a practice routine. Your routine should include the following steps:

a. Preparation
b. Warm-up (Be certain that your instrument is properly tuned)
c. Tone quality
d. Understanding the assignments from your teacher
e. Work on your assignments
f. Putting your instrument away properly

Most of these steps will sound familiar to you because they have already been discussed in Units I through VIII.

Practice time: The amount of time you practice each day is not so important as *how* you practice. But, you will have better results if you practice at the same hour each day. Practicing at the same time each day will make music more a part of your life. Do not continue to play when your embouchure is sore or tired, or when you are tired. It is better to have two good short practice sessions when you are fresh and alert, than one long session when you are tired.

Practice techniques: To make the first four steps work the best for you, you must have some practice techniques. This means that when you begin to practice you need to know how to practice your music in the best way. Here are some practice techniques that will work for you:

a. Be accurate. Learn the correct notes as soon as you can. Do not waste time practicing wrong notes.

b. Know the best fingerings. Use the fingering chart in this book. For special fingerings, study Unit XI. You will sound better and enjoy playing more when you know that you are using the best possible fingerings.

c. Be musical. Make sure that you are playing the correct rhythms, dynamics, and phrasing.

d. Develop good finger movement. Finger movement is usually called *technique.* Some of the ways that you can learn to develop a good technique are given below.

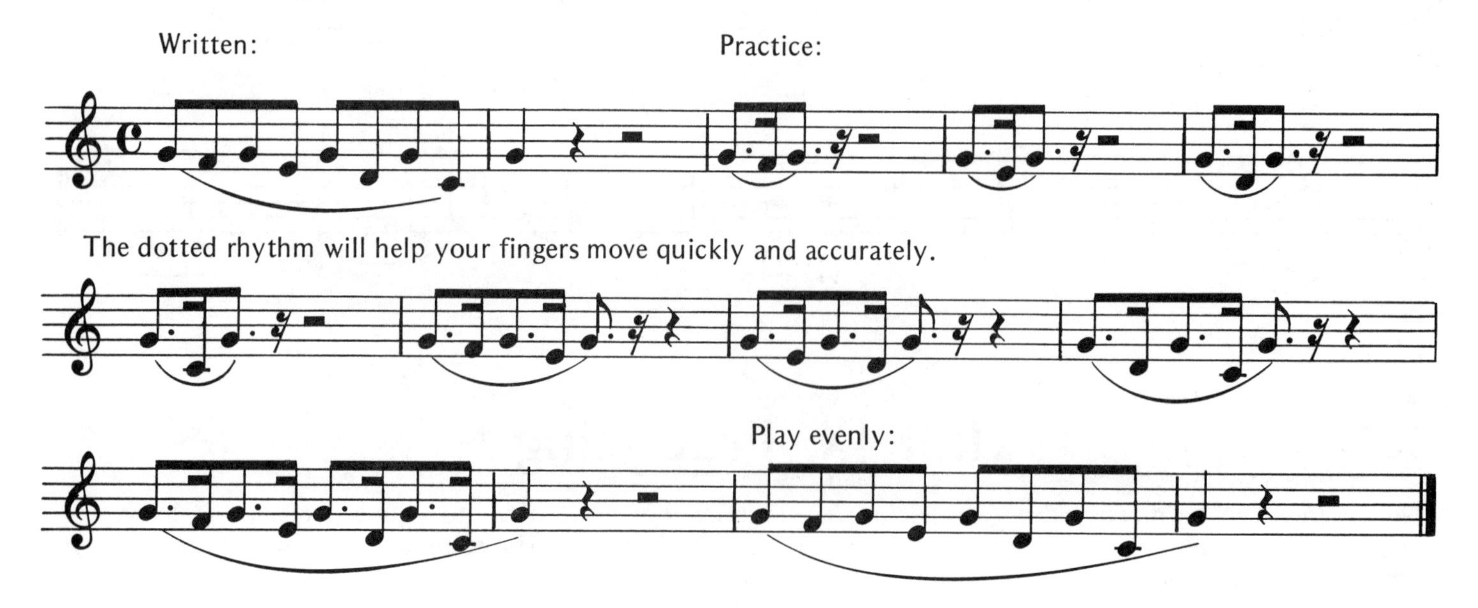
Written:
Practice:
The dotted rhythm will help your fingers move quickly and accurately.
Play evenly:

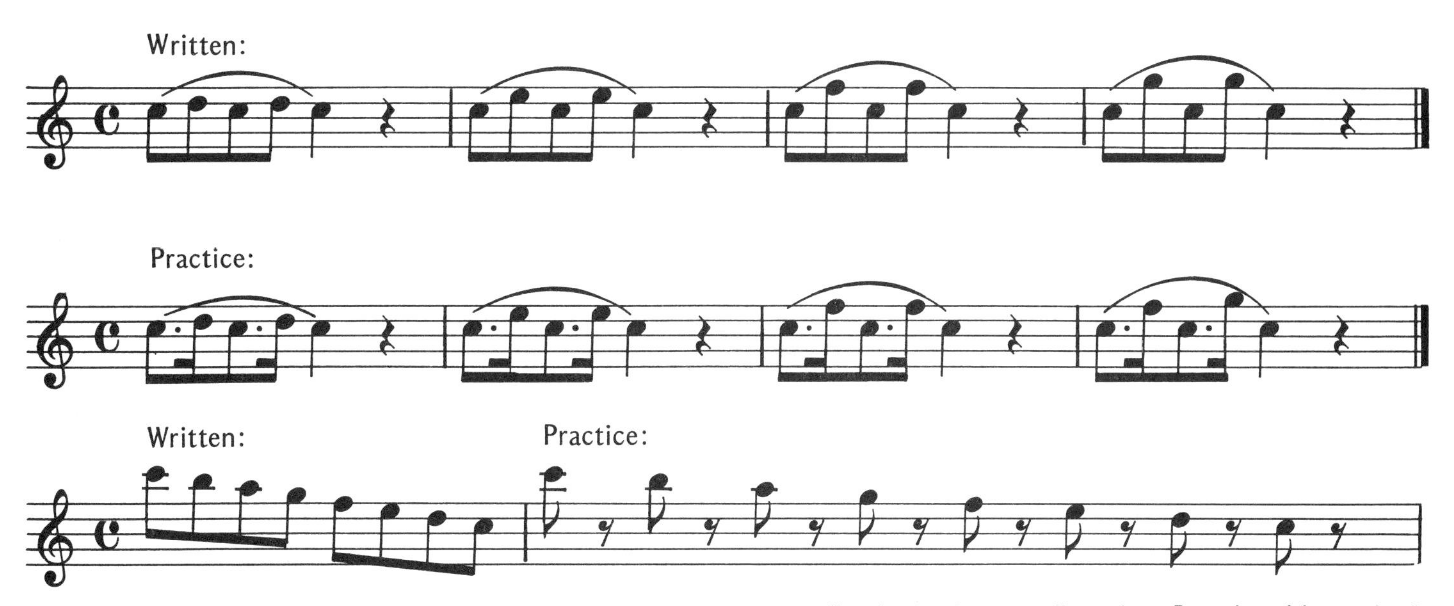

Practice this technique slowly. During the eighth rest go immediately to the next fingering. Practice this method in the examples below.

Go to the next fingering immediately during the rest.

Use these two practice techniques shown above for improving your playing of any music that you are trying to learn.

Unit X. Special Fingerings

Although you may know all or most of the basic fingerings for your instrument, there are times when special fingerings should be used. The best fingering will make it more enjoyable for you to play the saxophone. Also, you will sound better and play with more confidence. The most important special fingerings are shown below. Practice each example carefully so that you can remember to use a special fingering whenever it is the best choice.

Use the side fingering for C when you have B-C-B. Use it also for the B-C trill. It may also be used in the chromatic scale ascending.

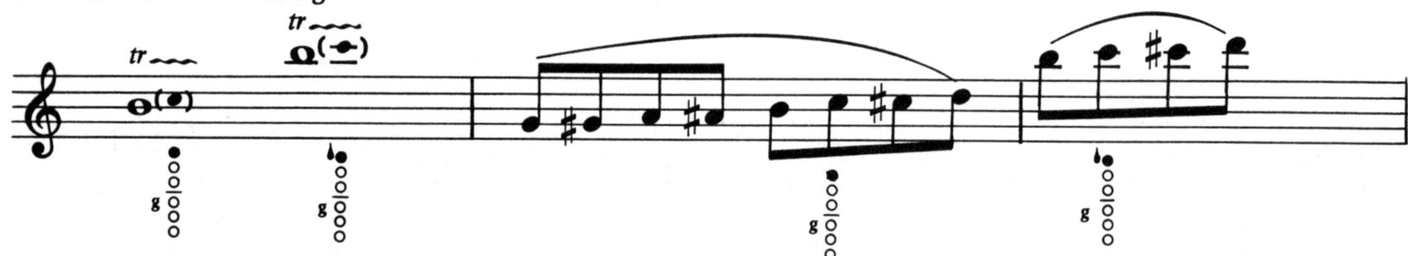

The side C fingering should not be used when the following note uses the right hand. Study the examples below.

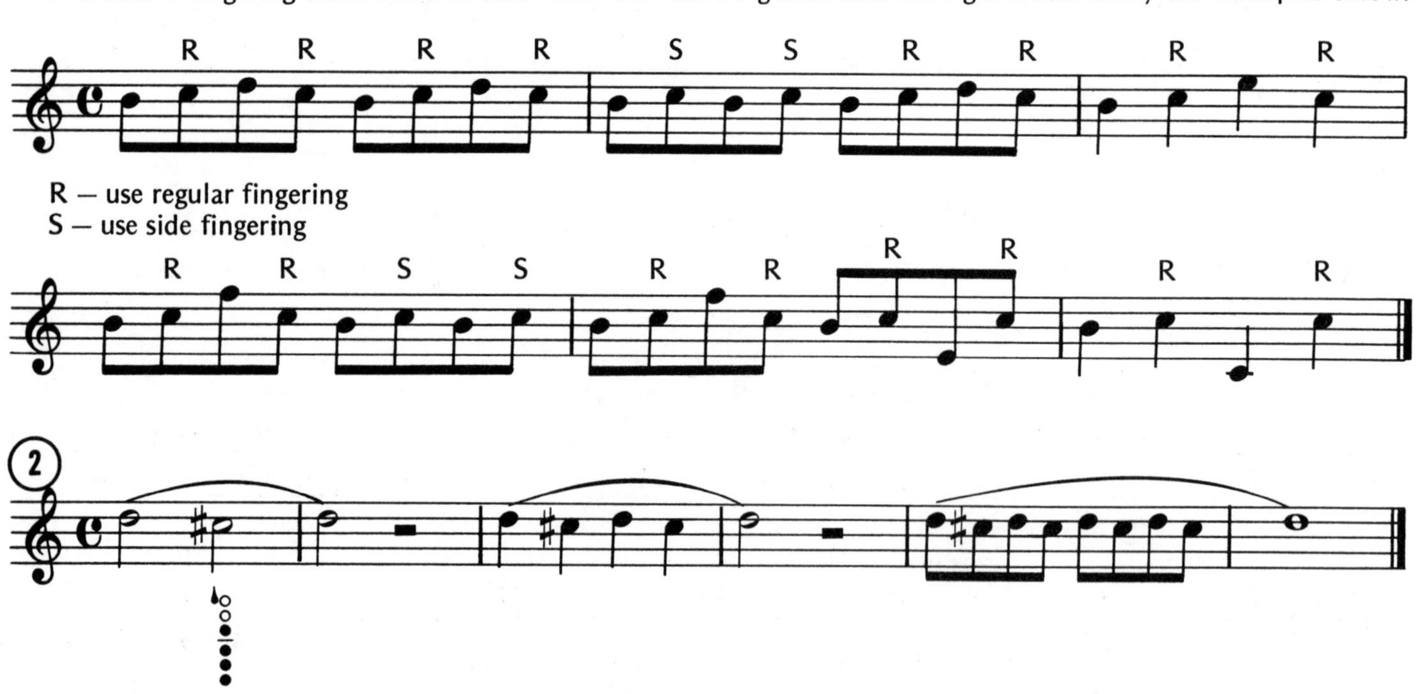

In these examples, use the fingerings shown for C-sharp (D-flat). The use of these special fingerings will give you a smoother connection between these two parts of the saxophone's range.

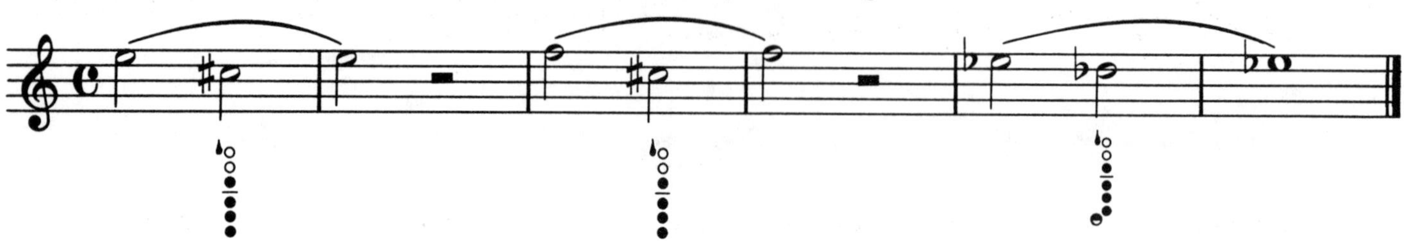

Use the side fingering for B-flat in all passages that move by a half-step to or from B. Also, use the side key in certain trills, as shown below.

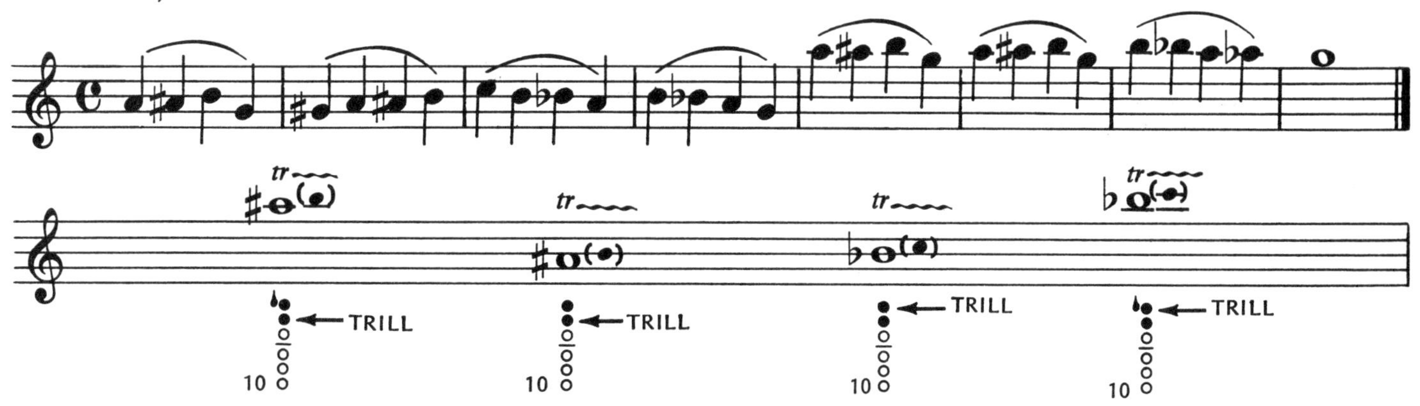

You may also play B-flat by having the index finger of your left hand cover the B key *plus* the small pearl below it (bis key). Use the bis fingering for B-flat in appropriate passages.

Use the bis fingering for B-flat in most other passages. Play and study the examples below.

Begin with the G-sharp key down and leave it down throughout.

Trills

A trill is an alternation between two notes. Always go to the scale degree above when a trill is indicated. Practice the following examples slowly and evenly.

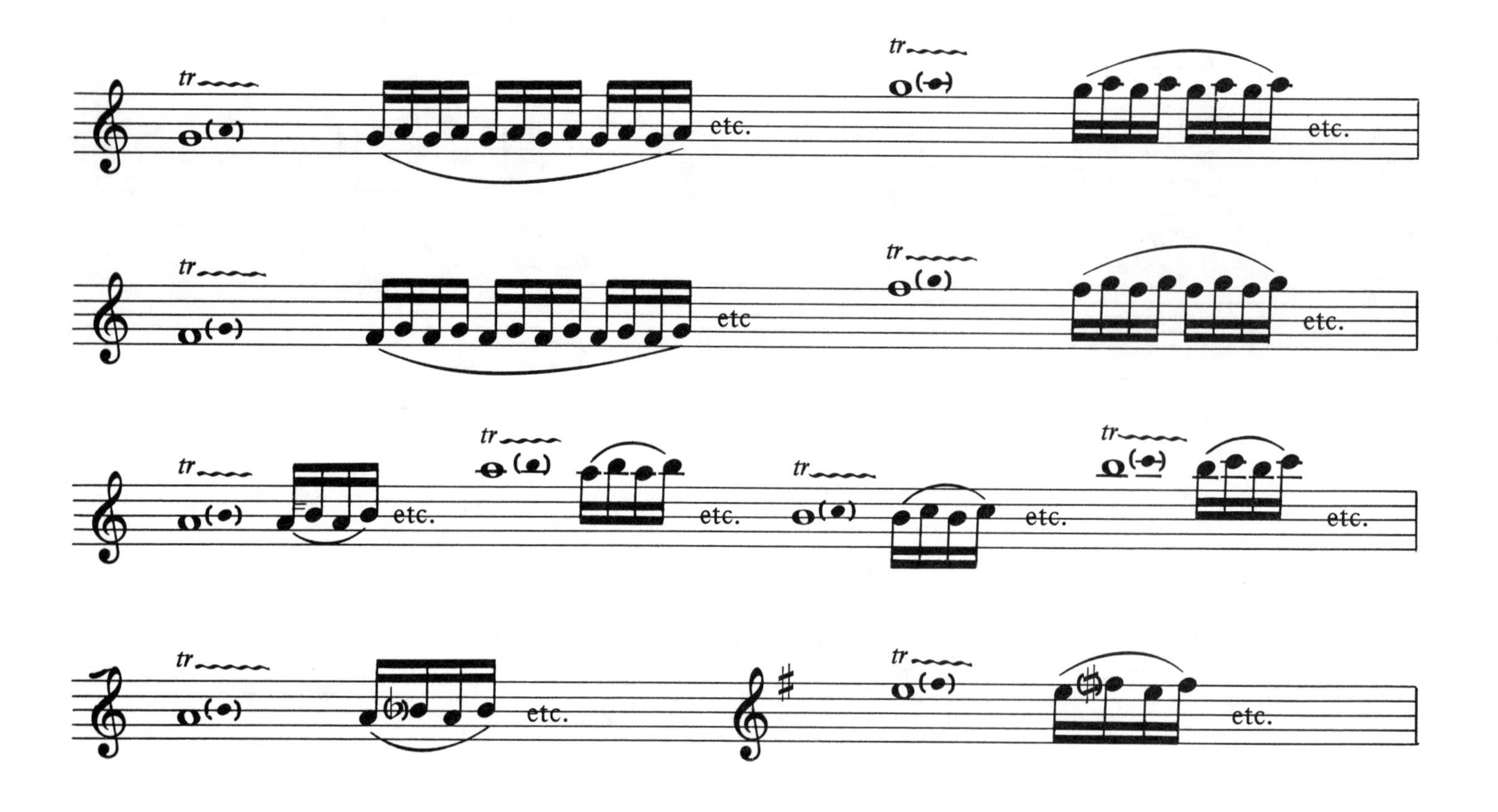

Sometimes the trill will indicate that a flat or sharp is to be used.

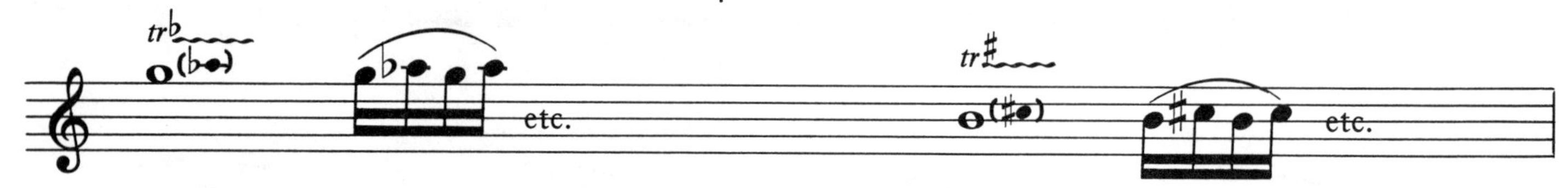

Unit XI. Selected Etudes

R. SCHUMANN
(1810-1856)

March

R. SCHUMANN
(1810-1856)

Bagatelle
BEETHOVEN
(1770-1827)
Allegretto
Andante
Op. 34, No. 21
TSCHAIKOWSKY
(1840-1893)
poco rit.
a tempo
rit.
Allegretto Grazioso
A. CALDARA
(1671-1763)
rit.
rit.

A. M. R. BARRET
(1804-1879)
Moderato
p
p
mf
f
f
p
mf
mp
p
f
A. M. R. BARRET
(1804-1879)
Moderato
mf
1
f
2
f
mp
ff
mf

Hunting Song

R. SCHUMANN
(1810 - 1856)

*Hunters' Chorus

C. M. VON WEBER
Arr. by EUGENE ROUSSEAU

*This solo, complete with piano accompaniment, is published by Belwin-Mills Publishing Corp., and is available through your music dealer.

*This solo, complete with piano accompaniment, is published by Belwin-Mills Publishing Corp., and is available through your music dealer.

*Spring

EDVARD GRIEG (1843 - 1907)
Arr. by EUGENE ROUSSEAU

*This solo, complete with piano accompaniment, is published by Belwin-Mills Publishing Corp., and is available through your music dealer.

*The Swan

C. SAINT–SAENS
Arr. by EUGENE ROUSSEAU

*This solo, complete with piano accompaniment, is published by Belwin-Mills Publishing Corp., and is available through your music dealer.

Saxophone Fingering Chart

When a number is given, refer to the picture of the Saxophone for additional keys to be pressed. When two notes are given together (F♯ and G♭) they are the same tone and, of course, played the same way.

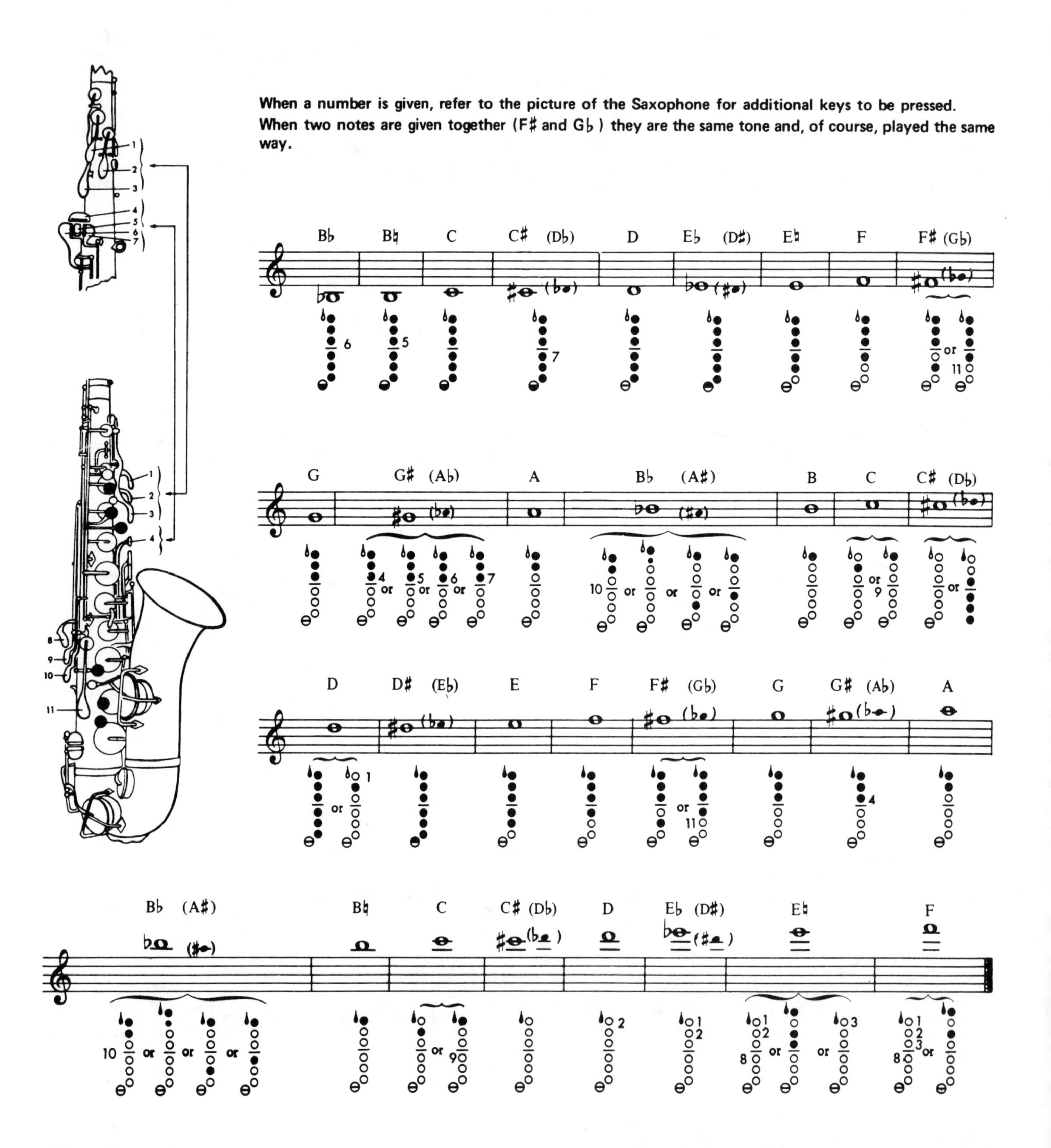